Dedicated to Mum and Dad

First published in 2015 by Scholastic Children's Books
Euston House, 24 Eversholt Street
London NW1 1DB
a division of Scholastic Ltd
www.scholastic.co.uk
London ~ New York ~ Toronto ~ Sydney ~ Auckland
Mexico City ~ New Delhi ~ Hong Kong

Text and illustration copyright © 2015 Jo Williamson

HB ISBN 978 - 1407 - 15275 - 2
PB ISBN 978 - 1407 - 15276 - 9

A very big **Woof** to all you dogs!

Here is my guide to help
you have some fun and
be happy in your new home...

Just don't tell those **humans!**

The first thing you need to do is choose a human to live with.

They can all look alike...

...but you will know when you have found the right one.

Just like I did.

In your new home you will realise that you can fall asleep anywhere

and you will soon...

...find your favourite place.

Remember to always say hello to your human in a friendly way.

And welcome any visitors...

...but be less friendly to strangers.

Your human will want you to be toilet trained...

Mine was very glad when I got the hang of it.

Always be ready for any food that may come along...

Your human will be pleased with your help to clean the floor.

To get extra treats, pretend that you have not been fed.

If that doesn't work...

...you may need to learn some new tricks.

paw   lie   twirl

sing   dance   balance

When playing ball, run straight back and drop it at your human's feet.

If they get bored, you could try a different game.

You will meet new neighbours...

...and make lots of friends.

Or sometimes not.

You will soon know what you like doing the most...

...and the least.

But you won't really care as long
as you are with your BEST friend.

And you will be very happy
in your new home.

Just like me.